901817775X

D0997160

Please return/renew this item by the last date shown.
Item may also be renewed by the internet*

https://library.eastriding.gov.uk

* Please note a PIN will be required to access this service
- this can be obtained from your library.

THANKS TO:
LAURENCE KING
DONALD DINWIDDIE

EDITED BY
NATASCHA BIEBOW AT
BLUE ELEPHANT STORYSHAPING
IN CONJUCNTION WITH
DONALD DINWIDDIE
AT L.K.P.

PRODUCTION
FELICITY AWDRY

DESIGN
VANESSA GREEN @
THE URBAN ANT

LITERARY AGENT
ELIZABETH SHEINKMAN. PFD

ANGUS HYLAND
Hamish & Alexander
X X X

LAURENCE KING

PUBLISHED IN 2020 by
LAURENCE KING PUBLISHING LTD.
361-373 CITY ROAD
LONDON EC1 1LR
TEL: + 44 20 7841 6900
www.laurenceking.com
enquiries @ laurenceking.com

A CATALOGUE RECORD OF THIS BOOK IS
AVAILABLE FROM THE BRITISH LIBRARY.

ISBN 978-1-78627-4908

Printed in China.

For Helen

Bob
Goes
POP!

Written and Illustrated by
Marion Deuchars

LAURENCE KING

"Hey Bob!
Have you seen the new artist in town?"
said Owl. "He's called Roy the Sculptor
and EVERYONE'S talking about him!"

"Roy WHO?"
Bob said. "But I'm
the BEST artist in town."

So Bob went to meet Roy.
He was a rather smug-looking blue parrot.

"Hello!" said Roy, "I hear you're an artist too.
What do you think of my fantastic sculpture?
I call it...
HAMMYbammyCHEESYbunny."

"Here's another. This one is called
GREENblobPAINTBRUSHsplob."

"And how about this one? My
SHUTTLEbuttle KNICKNOCKScuddle."

"Oh! But they're just ordinary objects except bigger," said Bob.

" **MY** SCULPTURES aren't ORDINARY! They're EXTRAORDINARY!

BESIDES, anyone can make a BORING PAINTING.

I BET you couldn't EVEN **MAKE** a SCULPTURE!" snapped Roy.

" It's EASY! I bet
you I CAN!"
said Bob.

The next day, Bob made his first sculpture.

"Ta-da!
I call it
DOTTYDOT BarkyBARK."

"NICE"

"But come and look at what Roy's just made!"

"I call it LICKlick SLURPYslurp," said Roy.

"Humph! It's just a big Lollipop," said Bob.

Bob tried again.
MY
BENDY yellow-
BELLIED nanas.

"Totally
bananas!"
said Bat.

"But come and look at what Roy's just made!"

The next day, Bob made another sculpture.

But so did Roy!

Bob tried again.

And so did Roy.

"So yolky!" smiled Owl.

Bob kept trying...

But Roy's sculptures really were EXTRAORDINARY...
Bob needed some new ideas.

That night he crept over to Roy's workshop.

"Just a tiny peek..."
he whispered.

The next day, Roy revealed a giant balloon dog
And Bob revealed...

an identical GIANT balloon dog!
"It's called...
BLOBBY DOG WOOF WOOF !"
they both said at the same time.

"That's MY idea!"
shouted Roy.

"YOU COPYCAT!"

Roy GRABBED Bob's Blobby.
They TUSTLED and TUMBLED until...

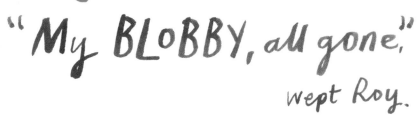

"My BLOBBY, all gone,"
wept Roy.

"I'm so sorry,"
sobbed Bob.

"I could make you a new one?
We could make it...together?"
pleaded Bob.

"Maybe..."
sniffed Roy.

"You can do the sculpting, and I can do the painting," said Bob.

"WHAT'S GOING ON in there?"

At last, Bob and Roy revealed their creation...
"WE call it...

BLOBBYDOG
WOOF WOOF WOW!"

"Now that really is EXTRA, EXTRA-ORDINARY!"
said Owl.

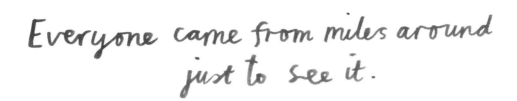

Everyone came from miles around
just to see it.

"Now we are BOTH the best artists in town!" said Bob.

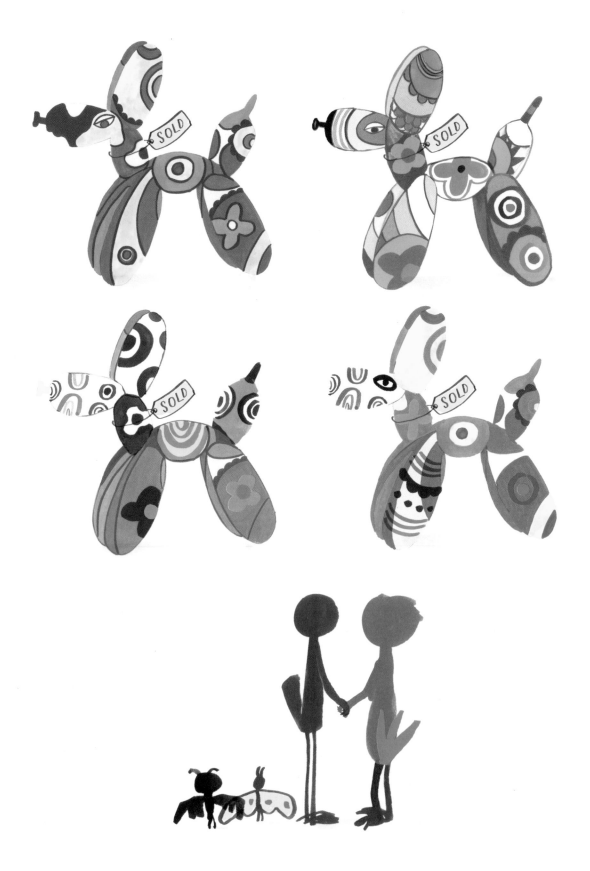

"And best of all, we're friends."

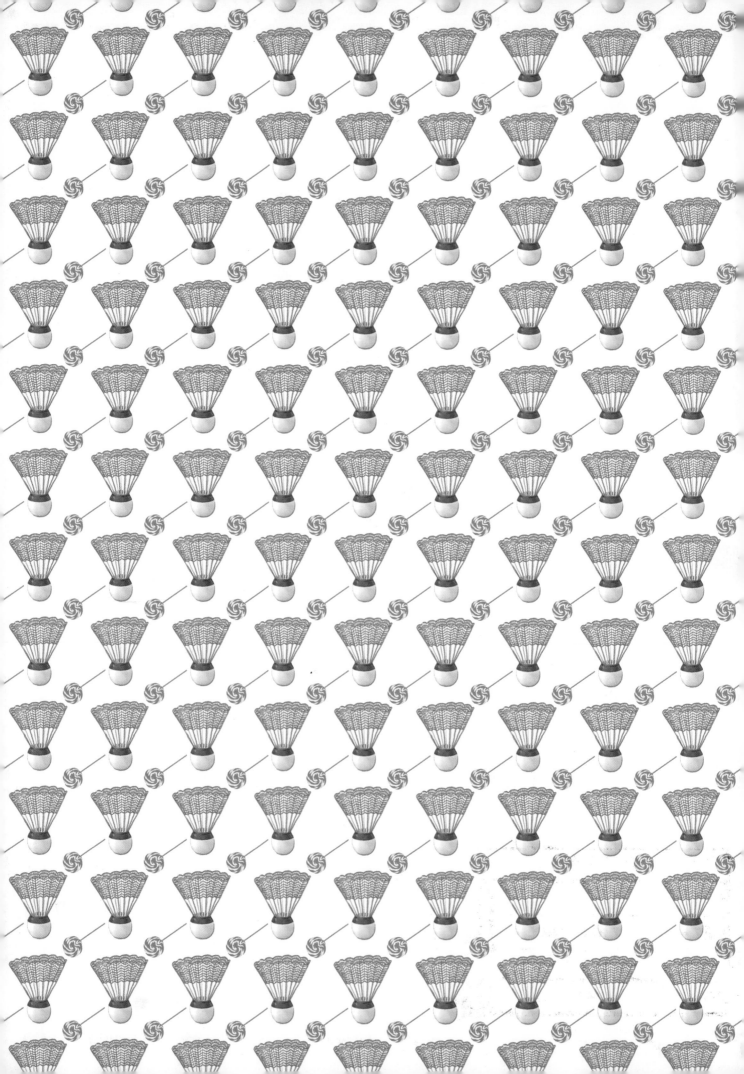